LOVE'S JOURNEY – EVEN IN WAR

M. A. Valdellon

Published by M. A. Valdellon
www.melissavaldellon.com

Cover design by Elena Lavrova

ISBN-13: 978-0692105993
ISBN-10: 0692105999

We don't even know how strong we are until we are forced to bring that hidden strength forward. In times of tragedy, of war, of necessity, people do amazing things. The human capacity for survival and renewal is awesome.

- Isabel Allende

CONTENTS

1

"Oh God, no."

Landon Scott couldn't believe his eyes. The dirty-blonde haired, green eyed man felt his shoulders slumping forward. His breath felt like it had been sucked from his lungs, and if it weren't for the fact that his wife, Jamie, was in his arms, he felt like he would have collapsed, his knees feeling like they could buckle from under him at any moment. Something was wrong. He couldn't have just been drafted. Others maybe, but not him. Oh please, not him. It was all too surreal. He saw strangers' names as they scrolled through the lists upon endless lists posted. He even caught Luke's name, as well as Hudson's and Adrian's, each guy another one of his former bandmates from another time, brothers by choice. But him?

And all he had to do was feel the woman in his arms crying her heart out and feel the cool sheet of paper in his hand to confirm in his heart that his senses weren't lying.

He automatically held Jamie tighter in his arms and started rocking her. "Shh, shh, Jamie," he murmured softly as he closed his eyes and held on to the woman. It was all he could think of to say, even as the world felt like it was shifting in a new direction, one he didn't recognize. "It'll all be all right. You'll see."

"No, it won't," she sobbed. "How can you say that? You're going off to war! I don't want you to go!"

"I know, sweetie. I don't want to go either, but duty calls," he sighed heavily, wishing it were only that simple.

She only cried harder.

"Hey, Landon. Hi, Jamie."

He opened his eyes and found himself looking at a familiar face. Smiling a little, Landon broke away from his wife long enough to clap Adrian on the back and give him a hug. "Hey, Sprout. Long time, no see, man," he said. "Hi, Katie," he greeted Adrian's longtime girlfriend, noting the redness in their eyes too. "How are you?"

"We could definitely be a lot better. God, Landon. Who would have thought that you guys would be going to fight in the war?"

Again, he felt Jamie give a shudder and he hugged her tight, offering what comfort he could.

"Obviously, none of us," Luke answered as he, Hudson, and Caleb joined the two youngest members of the once famous pop group, One Harmony.

The guys greeted each other with warm but saddened embraces as they met up all together for the first time in a long while, everyone brought together under strange circumstances outside their control to assemble at this nearest stadium to receive official notice.

There was Hudson Nelson, the eldest of the group by age and whose internal drive for perfection was often overlooked because of his goofy personality. Gone were the long locks he'd had when they'd all come together to perform on stages near and far. His dark brown hair was cut short, no longer hiding the warm, brown eyes that had made so many fans go crazy years ago.

Then there was Luke Thompson, easily the most light hearted of the group, always the social one trying to get everyone up and out for some kind of fun or mischief. His brown eyes normally twinkled with mirth – today, those eyes were muted and even almost seemed sunken in. The animated joy Landon and the world knew Luke for was gone for the time being, a somber figure here as a replacement.

The blue-eyed "baby" of the group, Adrian Roberts, had long since outgrown them all physically but they all still considered him to be the baby as the youngest of the five of them. His dirty blonde hair was all slicked back, and he'd grown out a beard and mustache since their boyhood days together.

Landon looked over to Caleb Young last. Even though he hadn't been the oldest one of the group, he had been the father figure for them all, pushing them all to do their best each and every moment they were together. Landon had to give Caleb the credit for being a big part of the creative force behind their group as their careers took off. And of course, his silky smooth voice to go along with their silky smooth choreographed moves hadn't hurt them one bit. Now though, he saw the absolute anguish in his friend's face.

"I don't know. Do you guys get a bad feeling about this?" Hudson asked.

Landon nodded. "This isn't right at all. I never thought we'd be brought together again in this kind of situation. Can you remember the last time we were here," he asked, waving an arm to indicate the stadium they were in. "We played to an audience of thousands. And now this," he gestured to the masses around them, a heavy, oppressive feeling in the air.

"Man, Caleb. You're so lucky you're not going."

"I can't lie and say that I'm not a little relieved. At the same time though, you guys don't know how guilty I feel for being the one left behind here. It's not fair to you guys at all that you *have* to go. I couldn't get you guys to do anything before, why should the government be able to now?" His friends all smiled weakly at his attempt at a joke. He sighed. "You guys are my brothers. I don't want to lose any of you," he said, emotion thick in his voice as he turned away so no one could meet his eyes.

"Well, now that we all have the official news, there's nothing left for us here. Shall we get together at my place? For old times sake, you know?" Luke asked.

With nothing better to do, the group agreed.

'So that officially makes it four out of the five members of One Harmony,' Landon thought to himself. 'Hudson, Luke, Adrian, and I. Who among us will make it back home after this war is done and over?' He shook his head, trying to clear it as he concentrated on following Adrian's car to Luke's, his left hand on the wheel and his right clutching Jamie's hand tightly for support.

"You'll be all right," Jamie said out loud, as if she

were reading his mind. "And so will the rest of the guys." But they both knew how flat and hopeless sounding her voice was even as she spoke.

Landon drew her hand to his lips. "Let's hope you're right," he replied, giving her a quick kiss.

- - -

"The mail's here," Jamie called.

"Anything good or happier by any chance?" Landon asked as he locked the door behind them once they were inside. The gathering at Luke's had been anything but fun, though they did reminisce plenty on the good times they had shared together in the past and then caught up on what they'd all done since their official split. With the majority of the group officially being deployed for war though, it was difficult to find any sort of relief from the somber feeling in the air.

"Well, there's a duplicate of your summons letter here, but there's also something addressed to me from the army," she said, frowning a little bit.

"What is it?" he asked, coming up behind her and wrapping his arms around her. He kissed her softly on the neck before resting his head on her shoulder so they could both read its contents.

Dr. Jamie Scott,

This letter serves as notification confirming your recall to active duty and call to assist in this third world war by providing your services in the medical field. This is a dark and troublesome time for all of us, and we understand how difficult this must be for you, but please understand that we need dedicated individuals such as yourself in times of such crisis.

Attached to this letter are instructions directing you to the closest base. Please report there by the date listed in those instructions. There, you will be given further instructions as to...

Landon felt icy hands clutch his heart as Jamie gave a whispered, "Oh, God. In looking for your name, we didn't even think to look for mine in those lists." The paper fell from her hands and slowly fluttered to the ground. Neither remembered her turning around, but the next thing they knew, they were both crying again, holding tightly onto each other as they let their tears mingle. "This wasn't supposed to happen," she sobbed. "I've already paid my dues!" she cried bitterly.

He could only keep crying.

2

"*Now boarding passengers in rows six through twenty-five. I repeat, we are now boarding passengers seated in rows six through twenty-five.*"

"Come on, sweetie," Landon urged his wife up onto her feet. "That's us."

"Landon, I don't want to go," Jamie answered quietly even as she followed him to queue up at the terminal gate, her hand trembling and icy in his. "I can't help this awful feeling like one of us isn't going to make it back."

Landon showed the flight attendant their tickets and walked on, all the while holding Jamie's hand gently in his. "Come on now," he said in a reassuring tone. "We've still got training to go through. With any luck, you and I will flunk out and miss the whole war entirely."

"Landon, this isn't a joking matter," she frowned.

"I know, I know," he sighed. "I'm sorry. But your mentioning such a premonition isn't making me feel any better either. I know it's not funny, but sometimes I can't help but think this is all some strange and twisted joke."

"Tell that to the people who are fighting already and losing their lives because of it."

"People are going to die anyway."

"And that's supposed to make it all better?"

"No, no, of course not," Landon defended quickly,

shaking his head. "It's just... I don't know. It's just not sinking in yet on some level."

Jamie silently agreed with that last statement and took her seat next to the window. Landon sat down only a moment later after placing their carry on above them, and instantly, their hands grasped each other's for comfort.

Ever since the news had come to the couple just days before, any sort of separation had been practically unbearable. The two had needed each other's touch and to hear each other's voice as much as they needed food and water to survive – they needed the physical reminders to know that this wasn't a dream.

And remind themselves that neither was alone.

The last couple of days had hardly been enough time to get everything done. Phone calls to family and friends had lasted forever as more tears were shed and good-byes were made. Arrangements had to be made for one of Jamie's friends to come by and check on the house once in awhile and to get the mail, seeing as he was the closest friend they had living nearby. Paperwork had to be filed for all the worst case scenario settings. Companies had to be called to have their services cut off until they returned... And who knew when that would be?

"The point is that we're together right now," he said, tightening his grip on his wife's hand as they settled on board the plane.

"Yeah. I suppose you're right. As long as we're together, nothing else matters, right?" she looked up into his eyes, needing his reassuring gaze.

"Exactly," he affirmed. A short silence fell upon

them when they realized that flight attendants were signaling for everyone's attention as they went over the emergency procedures. Jamie lay her head down on Lance's shoulder for the presentation and he gently leaned his head against hers. By the time the safety demonstration was over, they were already speeding down the tarmac, ready to fly high up in the clouds, turning the earth below them into a swirl of browns and greens.

"How are the guys?" she asked after a few minutes of silence had lapsed.

"Adrian and them?" he glanced over. "Just as good or bad as we are, depending on how you look at it" he admitted. "They're worried. Sad. Stressed. It's been good talking to them more again though, so at least that's been one good thing from this so far, and I think we'll at least be seeing a bit more of them for a few weeks yet. I think they said their instructions were to go to the same base we're going to." He smiled a little. "Talking to them though," he chuckled. "Some things just never change."

"Does that mean you guys may think about finally heading back to the studio after all this is said and done?" she teased.

"Oh, I don't know about that. Why gamble on trying to recreate something that did so well in the past? Our luck may have run out."

"Don't talk about luck, Landon. You guys have talent. That's worth more than luck any day."

"Says the woman who'd never heard of us or our music prior to meeting me," he joked, raising her hand to give it a tender kiss. "Besides, if it's not luck, then how would you explain me finding the most beautiful woman in the world to share my life with?"

Jamie blushed a little. "Fate, love. We were meant to be."

"Right, and I just happened to walk into the very café you chose to go to on your first day back as a civilian."

She smiled a little bit, her blue eyes twinkling with the love and affection she had for the green-eyed singer sitting next to her. "College and medical school and two tours of duty later, and I had no idea who the heck you were, having been cut off from the civilized world for so long."

"And that was certainly to my advantage. You had no pre-conceived notions of who I was leading up to our meeting."

"Ahh, yes, the moment you came up to me and asked to pay for my drink and asked me to join you at your table where you were sitting," her eyes lighting up fondly with the memory.

Landon squeezed his wife's hand lightly. No more words were needed at this moment. Right now, just sitting next to each other, her head on his shoulder and his head resting lightly on top of hers... It was enough.

3

The silence hung thick in the air as the assembly of people waited in a crowded, auditorium for someone to take the stage. Landon and Jamie sat together in the middle of the crowd, her hands wrapped tightly by his. Adrian was sitting at Landon's left, and Hudson and Luke were sitting in the row in front of them, a few seats down. No one was speaking, and the tension of the room weighed down heavily on them.

Then, the heavy sound of boots echoing from somewhere backstage signaled the imminent arrival of a man long before the audience saw him. A man dressed in brown fatigues crossed onto the stage and stopped upon reaching the middle. He walked slowly and deliberately, as he had been trained to do, but even from her vantage point, Jamie could see the tell-tale signs of fatigue in the man's face and demeanor.

The man took a moment before looking out into the crowd of people before him, the sea of faces of those individuals who had been brought into this war without a choice. He ignored the podium and the microphone just to his right and addressed the crowd as he was, his voice reaching everyone even in the back in the silence that blanketed them otherwise. "You are here today because of other people's choices. Now, it is not my position to say whether or not such a choice was right. It is not my position to explain why you have been asked to leave your work, your family and friends, your homes, your very lives as you've known it to be to come here while others are left behind. It is not my position to tell you that you should or shouldn't be scared, should or shouldn't be angry, should or shouldn't be unhappy with this situation. It is not my position to say whether or not this war is justified in the first place. I am here, however, for the same reason you are here – to serve this country of ours, to protect the loved ones that we have left behind, and to safeguard the better future we hope will come soon."

He paused for a little bit, gauging the emotions running across the faces in front of him. There was some curiosity and a touch of inspiration here and there, some wariness, some sadness, and a lot of fear. He gave a mental sigh before his mouth opened to speak again.

"I am Major Harper and I will be in command during your time here in training. Now, the training you will be undertaking here will be unlike anything most of you have ever been through. Our goal is simple – to get you as physically and mentally prepared as possible in one month's time so that we can get you over to where you are needed most. Immediately following this meeting, you will be split up to start your training. Most of you will be following Sergeant Doneza to get started with basic training," he announced, pointing to the man on his right. "I understand there are individuals here too who have been trained to serve in other ways. Those doctors, nurses, aides, and other medical personnel are to follow Sergeant Timmes," he indicated to the man on his left. "To get up to speed on the types of situations and conditions you will be faced with."

Major Harper glanced again over the crowd and noticed the increase in worry he saw on the faces. "Ladies and gentlemen, this is a strange time we're living in right now. I don't think there are any of us here in this room that grew up thinking we'd be witness to a period where so much is at stake. The fact is, however, that we are here, right now. What you start today, what you are undertaking here may very well go on to influence the lives of everyone in this world. It would serve you best to remember that, that even in war, there is some good to attain to, and that we are attempting to make the world a better, safer place for everyone in the long run." He paused a moment to let that statement sink and settle in. "Sergeant Doneza, Sergeant Timmes, if you will gather your respective groups please."

The heavy silence of the hall vanished as everyone stood up, metal scraping on the floor as chairs were moved aside. Jamie clutched tight to Landon's hand, even as he started to move away towards his left to join the others for basic training. Landon was squeezing her hand just as hard, but turning back to her, he gave her hand a pat with his left hand, smiling and radiating his love for her through his eyes. Both took heart in knowing that at least this separation was temporary, and Jamie just gave a small nod and smile. They eased the tension in their hands and let the other's hand slip away. "I'll see you tonight," he said as he moved again, away from her.

"Tonight," she echoed with one last glance to her husband before joining the smaller group of people over to the right of the stage.

4

"How are you doing?"

Jamie looked up from her cramped desk to find Landon standing in the doorway of the temporary building she had called home for the last three weeks. The other women she was living with smiled and waved in his direction before turning back to their own work. Jamie allowed a smile to come to her face. "I'm good now that you're here."

He crossed the floor and came to stand behind her chair, stooping down to give her a hug. "Hanging in there all right?"

"I should be asking you that. How was today's training?"

He sighed. "Rough. Like always. It's hard, you know, going through all that physical fitness training for so many different scenarios and trying to cram it all in before we're shipped out next week. I'm not as young as I used to be, when we were rehearsing all our complicated dance routines before. There was at least music to work with then too. And we definitely didn't have to deal with the mental aspect of everything. It's like a crash course in psychology or something."

"Which you never took either," she smiled. "You're so old, grandpa," she joked, reaching up to pat him on the cheek in mocking comfort. "Come on. Let's go get something to eat."

"You read my mind," he smiled. He grabbed her hand and the two walked over to the mess hall. After grabbing a couple of trays, they found themselves sitting at the end of one table across from each other. "So really, are your courses going okay?"

"All the refreshers I've had to do take make sure I don't buckle under pressure?" she joked across the table to her husband.

"Something like that," he grinned back as he reached across the table to grasp onto one of her hands.

"They're not bad, you know. We do take continuing education courses for a reason so it's not completely new. We've been running through different scenarios though, and a lot of it is trying to deal with priorities and such and suggestions on how to be flexible. If anything else, I know there's going to be a lot more blood and guts once we get down there than what I've gotten used to."

"You're a surgeon! Shouldn't you already be used to the blood and gore?"

"Used to it now that I only have one patient to work on at a time in a sterile environment and where I have the proper resources. I don't normally have mass surgeries going on every day or even have to think of the potential to be in that situation, you know. This could be very different, depending on the location we're being sent to."

He nodded his head an agreement and put a spoonful of the mashed potatoes he'd gotten into his mouth.

"You know, you two are so lucky to have each

other right now," Luke said as he, Hudson, and Adrian joined the couple at the table, their trays also laden with food.

"Missing your ladies back home?" Jamie asked, already knowing the answer.

Adrian nodded. "But I did get a note from Katie today. She's doing well and she says hi to everyone. I suspect it's the last letter I'll be getting from her in awhile though. God, what's the likelihood that this war will end before we ship out next week?"

"You want the real stats? Probably nill," Hudson replied with a sigh, his mood uncharacteristically gloomy as he pushed the food around on his plate for a bit before taking a bite.

"Well isn't that the saddest thing I've heard come out of your mouth in a long while," Jamie said. "Cheer up, old man. At least you're not going into this one alone."

"She's right, you know," Landon said as he squeezed Jamie's hand a little bit again. "We're here together, now, right this moment. Let's be thankful for that at least."

Hudson nodded, a small smile coming onto his face. "I know. It's just weird, being all together but not being all together, you know?"

"Together as in here we are, minus Caleb but with Jamie. And we're not on stage but instead in a cafeteria in the middle of nowhere together?" The group looked at Luke. "What?"

Adrian just smiled. "I still find it very amusing when the words coming out of your mouth make sense."

"Oh, shut your gabber, Sprout. We were all

thinking the same thing."

The group of five friends laughed, easing the tension for a moment and leaving them thankful that there were still some things in the world that could leave them laughing. Landon glanced over at Jamie and smiled. "I love you," he murmured as the others continued to gang up on Luke.

Jamie looked back into the eyes of the man she loved and saw the love radiating out towards her. "I love you too," she said in return, squeezing his hand a little to emphasize her words. "We're going to pull out of this one together, all right?"

He answered with a smile and a kiss to her hand, sending her heart jumping with joy.

5

Jamie stood outside the guys' cabin and knocked. "Female present! Are you guys decent?"

"Jamie?" came a muffled sound from the other side of the door.

She laughed. "Who else would it be, silly?" She recognized Landon's voice telling her to hold on even as sounds of closets slamming shut and furniture moving around had Jamie cocking an eyebrow as she waited for a few moments before the door swung open. "Everything all right in here?" she asked with a grin as she looked past Landon's shoulder to see the other guys in the room calmly laying on their beds or, in Hudson's case, standing at his wardrobe mirror addressing his hair. Adrian was even whistling a tune to himself as he lay there, flipping through a magazine. "At ease, gentlemen," she teased as they said their respective hellos to her. "What was going on in here just now?"

"And what makes you think anything was happening?" Landon asked her, giving her his best innocent look.

She had to laugh. "Call it intuition. Let me guess, you guys are trying to dig yourselves out of this joint before we leave tomorrow."

"Hey, now why didn't we think of that?" Luke exclaimed. "If we start now, we could probably make it!"

"Yeah right. It's a little too late I think. If we start now, I think the furthest we'd get would be the mess hall, and that's not far at all," Hudson pointed out.

"So we'll shoot for the mess hall then. No one would think to find us there tomorrow!"

Jamie laughed. "The way you guys eat, I think that's one of the first places they'd look if you weren't around for roll call. Anyway, fine, if you guys don't want to tell me what's going on, I'll let you guys off the hook for now. Landon, come walk with me?" she turned her attention to her husband and held out a hand to him.

"I'd love to," came the reply as he took her hand and stepped out into the evening, the two of them ignoring the catcalls and teasing coming from the temporary building behind them. As soon as they were a good distance away from the building, Landon turned to the woman next to him. "So to what do I owe the pleasure of this little after dinner stroll?"

"Oh, nothing special. I just wanted to take a walk."

"And talk…" he added, finally commenting on the worry he'd noticed on her face earlier, despite the lightheartedness from their interactions just now.

She nodded. "And talk," she agreed quietly before giving a sigh. "Landon, I'm scared. If I was scared before, it's nothing compared to what I'm feeling right now. I can't believe we're actually leaving tomorrow."

He gave her hand a gentle squeeze. "I know. It's

pretty unbelievable. We've been here for a month training for this war, or re-training in your case, but it still hasn't seemed real, none of it really. This still just feels more like play than actual practice and preparation than anything else."

"But that's the thing. It was all preparation and training with real equipment, real guns for something that is totally real and going on elsewhere in the world as we speak. Today, we're in the US. Tomorrow, we'll be only God knows where with combat right around the corner. Tomorrow, a different destiny awaits, and it won't be like anything we could have dreamed."

"So what's the biggest thing you're worried about right now?" Landon asked, knowing her well enough to see that there was something at the root of her troubles.

Jamie sighed. "That whole feeling like something terrible is going to happen, it hasn't gone away, Landon, not since I first saw your name posted on that bulletin board when we were still back home."

"Your intuition again? You just had that earlier when you were getting me away from the guys, Jamie."

She smiled at his attempt to make the topic lighter. "That was different! I was teasing you then because you all had those innocent looks on your faces that showed you were clearly hiding something. This other feeling though?" Jamie gave an exasperated sight. "It's real. I can feel it deep in here," she said, placing a hand on her chest. "And it's terrifying me. I don't like knowing that the future is so uncertain. I don't like going into this knowing that one day, one of the guys might not come back, that maybe it will be you or maybe even I who won't be coming back. I can't make believe that that isn't a possible scenario just as much as I can't make believe we're actually leaving in the morning and heading into actual combat zones. Landon, I've been in difficult situations before and I know I can handle my own, but just knowing that this time you and the guys are there adds another level to this mess and makes things that much more different and difficult now for me. I have something to lose this time, and I definitely don't want to be losing you!" she exclaimed, finally letting the tears that she'd been holding back start slipping down her face.

"Hey, come here," he said, drawing her into his arms as the tears came and her body shook with her sobbing. "It's okay, sweetie, it'll be okay," he whispered as he rubbed her back trying to give her the support she needed.

"But you don't know that!" she protested.

Landon closed his eyes and gave a small sigh. "All right, no, I don't know for sure that things will be okay. I can't guarantee it or promise it, but I can try to believe it, Jamie. I've got to hope that this will all turn out okay, that come the end of each day we're away from our home, you'll be there for me and I'll be there for you. You and I, we're a team. We've committed to living with and loving each other day by day, and that's not going to change even if we're somewhere half a world away. We're in this thing together, love, and I'm not going to leave you willingly, you hear me?" he asked as he kissed her on the head.

Jamie clung onto him tighter, not wanting to ever let him go. "I hear you," she whispered, praying with all her might that everything would turn out fine in the end.

6

Jamie was humming a little tune to herself at her desk, flipping through the pages of one of her old anatomy textbooks that she'd brought along with her and jotting down a few points for herself on the legal pad next to her. Landon stood in the doorway of the makeshift tent she was sharing with a few others and indicated to them to just ignore him and not let Jamie know he was there either. He was content to just stand there and look at the love of his life – moments like these were just too few and far in between for him and that much more precious knowing that at any moment, it could all just as easily be lost in this war.

He smiled as he heard her start singing a few words under her breath, recognizing the lyrics to one of the songs he used to sing with the guys when they still toured what felt like ages ago. It was one of their more happy, upbeat tunes and still, he didn't move from his spot. The reason for his coming, for searching her out was still in his hands, but he knew that it could wait. For now, he just wanted to memorize the look of her again, etching that image of her in his mind. They'd been lucky thus far, being stationed at the same base since they were married. And it was even better and easier having the other guys share a tent with him, too. He tried to keep these comforts in mind, knowing that the future may not always be as great as they were now.

A few minutes later, Jamie sat back from the desk she'd been hunching over and tipped her chair back, rolling her head from side to side to ease the tension in her neck. Turning her head to the left, she spotted Landon in the doorway and almost fell over in her chair. "Landon! How long have you been standing there?" she exclaimed as everyone else in the room started chuckling.

"Long enough to know you still know at least one of our songs by heart," he teased as he came over and gave her a soft kiss. "You could have sung back up for us."

"Thanks, but no thanks. I know what my talents are and singing out loud, especially in front of people, isn't one of them," she smiled. "And for the sake of everyone's ears, I'm glad. So what brings you here?"

Landon kept smiling but she noticed that a little bit of the sparkle dimmed from his eyes as he brought over an unoccupied chair over to sit next to her. "The guys wanted me to give you these," he said, placing the envelopes he had in his hand onto the desk in front of her.

She looked at the pile curiously and picked one of the envelopes up. Slowly, realization dawned on her as she saw the names and addresses written in the guys' handwriting as she quickly looked through the rest of the pile and saw more of the same. "Landon?"

"They're just in case, Jamie," he started, trying to soothe the worry that was beginning to creep into her eyes. "We're going on our first extended excursion tomorrow to check on some old ruins and make sure that it and the surrounding areas are clear."

"Landon," she said in a low voice. "These are all letters from the guys to their loved ones back home. You don't think something's going to happen, do you?"

He sighed and took her left hand into his right and squeezed it gently. "I could lie and say no, but the truth is that I don't know. We're in the middle of a war zone and we never know what'll happen in the next hour, much less the next day. As I said, the letters are just in case the guys don't make it back. You'll be safe here on base so if anything happens, at least they'll feel better knowing that you have those letters."

"But..." She turned her eyes back on him and couldn't find the words to say. Being here was one thing already, but to add to the fact that even the guys knew that their futures weren't guaranteed... She felt a wave of hopelessness rising up in her and she found understanding gazing into his eyes, those green eyes that knew her best. It took her a few moments to fight against that feeling of despair, which was becoming all too familiar this time around, knowing that it wouldn't do anyone any good. In the end, she was able to calm her heart down for a little bit. Sighing quietly, she nodded. "I'll hold onto these for the guys then," she said as she took the pile and placed it in one desk drawer.

He gave a small smile and brought her hand up to his lips for another kiss. "Thank you."

She nodded again and gave his hand a squeeze before leaning over to give him a proper kiss. "Just watch over yourselves while you're gone, that's all I ask," she requested as she leaned her forehead against his.

"We will, I can promise you that." Landon closed his eyes and gave a small sigh. 'God please, if it is at all possible, please, please let us all get home safely after all this is done. Please, God...'

7

"Are you all right?" Adrian asked as he turned to look over at Landon. "You're not looking too good there."

"Just nerves," Landon replied, trying to shake off the uneasy feeling he had as the two made their ways over to the small airstrip. "You'd think this would get easier the longer we've been here and we'd be used to this by now," he muttered.

"Get used to going out every day into battle strapped down with all this gear?" Hudson asked as he shifted the pack on his shoulders. "I think not. I feel like a camel."

Luke nodded his head in agreement. "Yeah, but at least we got the gear to protect us. I don't even want to think of how many close calls we've been in since we've been here."

"Too true," Landon said. "We've been here now for how many months and there's still no end in sight it seems."

Adrian lightly punched Landon on the arm. "Don't worry. It will all have to end sometime."

The four of them had truly been lucky so far, being placed together more often than not. Sure, they'd endured a fair amount of teasing from the other soldiers here based on their history of being pop idols in the past and the fun times they must have had or the trouble they found themselves in.

Questions had been fielded about a possible reunion tour after the war, and they'd laughed it off, reminding everyone that they were focusing on taking it day by day, just like them. And in the end, they'd shown that they were here working as hard as everyone else, and with that, the teasing had calmed down.

The group now joined the other soldiers standing outside one of the cargo helicopters.

"Soldiers, it looks like we'll be heading out into the mountains some forty-five minutes to an hour from here," the commanding officer briefed. Landon recalled that the man had introduced himself as Major Leahy, a stocky man with a brusque manner. "One of our satellite stations has been attacked and we're going in to bring fresh supplies to our troops based there and bring the wounded back here for evaluation and treatment. Now I've been informed that a temporary ceasefire has been called to allow for this exchange and it's been calm, but I don't need to remind you lot that the situation can change at any given moment. As always, be prepared for the worst. We'll be flying out in ten minutes. Any questions?"

When no one said anything, they were dismissed and all spent the next few minutes finishing their various preparations before leaving for another excursion. Landon smiled as Adrian fished something out of his pocket and beckoned to the others. "Hacky sack?"

"Tradition is tradition," Luke said as Adrian tossed the beanbag over.

Jamie stood back for a minute to watch them play

before she made her presence known.

"Joining in?" Hudson asked, being the first to spot her.

"Sure," she replied as she took a spot between him and Landon.

A few more moments passed along with a few laughs before a warning was given to let the guys know they'd be leaving soon. With one last kick, Hudson hit the small bean bag neatly into Adrian's waiting hand.

"And now for the latest tradition, hand them over boys," Jamie announced with hand open and ready.

"And here I thought you were just hanging out," Landon teased as the other guys gave her their daily envelopes.

"Yeah right, not when I have work to be doing and a surgery room to prep for from the sound of things," she grinned back. "Anyway, I knew you guys wouldn't leave without giving me these."

"You know us too well," Luke said as he gave her a hug. "Thanks, Jamie."

"Anytime. You just watch it out there and I'll keep praying I never have to send these or the rest of the bundle back in my desk."

"We'll be careful," Hudson grinned as he shouldered his pack and headed towards the helicopter with Adrian after both had given her hugs as well.

"You too, okay?" Jamie asked as she turned to hug Landon tight.

"I will. We'll be back soon. I love you," he said as he gave her a quick kiss.

"I love you too. I'll see you later!" she said as their hands slipped apart. He gave her one last wink and headed off to join his friends onboard. She smiled and then turned to head back to the medical area for another round of checking in with some of the recovering patients.

- - -

"Is that the last of it?" one of the majors asked as Landon stepped away from the helicopter with another three-gallon container of water hoisted onto one shoulder.

"Yes, sir, this is the last of it."

"All right, start loading up the wounded," he barked out to a group of his soldiers who'd been waiting for that command.

Even as he made his way over to the building which, in times past, had served as a small grade school but now served as a sort of command center for the troops based here, Landon curiously watched as a handful of soldiers were lifted up onto the bed of the helicopter.

"Nothing major," Adrian said as he moved to walk with Landon and followed his friend's gaze. "They're lucky. Only a few bullet wounds and a broken bone here and there."

"Let's hope we all stay that lucky," he said as he moved indoors and put the water down against one wall with the other supplies. Adrian agreed as the two joined the rest of their team in another room.

They had just finished refreshing themselves with some water when Major Leahy strode into the room. He took a quick look around and called out for some of the men. "Hansen, Nelson, Thompson, Moreno. Major Brunner here has requested that we aid him in doing a quick scan of the surrounding area, and I need you four to join with the first patrol car to do just that. Roberts, Scott, Stokes, you three go with the second unit. The rest of you, I need you in the next room please."

The soldiers in the room split up with half the group heading outside to where a couple of trucks stood idling. Landon joined his comrades in the bed of the second truck and quick introductions were given as the two troops familiarized themselves with each other. "Hey, you're those One Harmony guys, aren't you?" one soldier who'd introduced himself as Jeremiah asked as the truck started to move forward after he'd taken a closer look at Adrian and Landon.

Landon shrugged. "No denying it here," he said as Adrian nodded his head.

Jeremiah let out a low whistle and grinned. "Man, my girlfriend will never believe this, that I met you guys! She was a huge fan of yours when you guys were still touring. You guys still do that?"

"Tour? Not so much recently. We've kinda been taking a break from that to do our own thing."

"What about the future?" another soldier asked, this time a redhead named Shane.

"Once we get out of this war? Who knows? It'd be nice to get together under non-war conditions, but if that leads to us collaborating again and going back into the music world? We'll see."

Landon nodded with Adrian's comment. "We're

just taking it one day at a time," repeating the same story they'd given anytime they'd been asked since being recruited.

"Aren't we all?" Jeremiah added before he started rummaging around in his pockets for something. "Hey, I know you must get this all the time, but would you mind if I got your autographs? I'm serious, my girl back home would be so happy," he said as he drew out a piece of paper and a pen.

Grinning, Adrian took the materials and prepared to write a little note. "What's her name?"

"Theresa."

As Adrian wrote down a few words, keeping mind of the jostling going on as their truck labored on, Landon looked back over at Shane and Jeremiah. "So how long have you guys been here?"

"Eight months, twelve days, and some ten hours, give or take a few minutes," came the reply.

Adrian glanced up quickly. "Keeping track that closely?"

Shane sighed. "Every minute I'm here is another minute I'm missing out on my baby girl's life. My wife, her name's Amie, gave birth to our first child the day before we were shipped out. I had one day to hold Caitlyn in my arms and the next day, I was gone."

"Ouch, sorry man," Landon said, not knowing what else to say.

"And can I say it again, you're lucky to at least have your wife nearby," came from Landon's right and he looked over at Frank Stokes, a soldier from the troop both Landon and Adrian were in.

"Your wife's here?" Jeremiah asked. "Wait, hold

that thought. You're married?"

Landon laughed as he took the pen and paper from Adrian's offered hand. "It's one of the things that happened to me since we all split to do our thing. Jamie's a surgeon. She did a couple tours with the army after medical school and is now helping out at the medic base we're stationed at."

"We couldn't all stay bachelors forever. Even us boyband guys need to grow up one day," Adrian laughed, seeing the still incredulous look on Jeremiah's face.

"Yeah, and the day that you grow up will be the day I go up into space," Landon joked.

Laughter eased a little bit of the tension that was present whenever the guys weren't safely at base, but it helped. Light conversation and a fair amount of soldierly teasing in that truck kept the morale high as their eyes continuously scanned the surrounding forest and mountain passes for any sign of the enemy.

A couple of hours later, the two trucks were well on their way to the base. "Another ten minutes and we'll be back," Shane announced as he spotted a familiar marker on the road.

"Things looking good up there?" Jeremiah called up to the truck ahead of them above the noise of the two engines.

"All good," they heard Luke's voice call back to them. "You guys okay back there?"

Jeremiah was about to yell back in confirmation when suddenly, an explosion from right next to that first truck caused dirt and debris to fly.

The men in Landon's truck instinctively ducked

and covered the backs of their heads and necks as the dirt began to rain down on them. Another explosion behind their truck left the five guys in that truck bed coughing and swearing as the truck stalled.

Landon glanced over at Adrian, green eyes meeting blue ones as dust and an unnatural silence settled around them. "Everyone all right in here?" he asked. The men around him let him know they were all okay, but what relief they had from that knowledge was short lived as triumphant shouting was heard getting closer to the two stalled trucks shortly before a round of gunfire crackled through the air.

"We're under attack! Everyone down!" Shane screamed as he pointed his gun out over the side of the truck and took aim at the first enemy he spotted rushing towards them.

Landon flattened himself as best he could in the awkward confines of the truck bed with all their gear and fired his rifle at another man who was screaming as he ran towards them with his gun blaring. Landon didn't even wait for that man to be completely down before his eyes were scanning the rest of the scene for anyone else coming. "You still have my letter, Sprout?"

Adrian grunted as he touched the pocket right above his heart, his eyes roving the landscape around them for another hostile enemy. "Naturally."

"Good. Keep that safe and tell her I love her, will you?"

"Tell her yourself, Landon. We'll get out of this one yet," Adrian grinned as he fired a shot to his right.

The attack was brief and over in less than five minutes. There had only been a handful or so of guerilla fighters and they'd been ill-equipped at that. After letting a couple more tense, silent minutes pass by, Jeremiah slowly eased himself up from the crouched position he'd forced himself into and the others followed suit. "We all right in here?"

"All fine, it looks like," Frank commented. "What about the other truck?"

"Luke? Hudson? Everyone okay there?" Adrian called out to the others.

"A little help would be good!" a voice called back. "Our driver's out and we've got a couple of bad injuries here."

Immediately, the five soldiers and their driver jumped out of the truck and went to where the other truck had swerved off the road ahead of them and partially into a ditch off the side of the road. "Shit," Landon vaguely heard Frank say as they saw how badly damaged the truck had been by the blast.

"Oh God, Luke?" Landon couldn't help the panic from entering his voice, his mind not seeing how anyone could have survived that kind of hit.

"Hudson!" Adrian screamed from right next to him as the two rushed forward to see if their friends were all right.

"Talk to me Dwayne, what have we got?" Shane asked as they approached.

A black haired man shook his head at him. "The driver's dead, killed by that IED likely, and RJ, Hudson, and Louis here are pretty close to saying hi to death too. They were sitting on the side of the truck that got hit."

It was Adrian's turn to swear as he maneuvered his way onto the truck with Landon right behind him. "Hudson, hang on buddy, you hear me? We got you and we're getting you out!" he said as he got some bandages out from his vest and began to apply them to his friend, even though he didn't respond.

Landon tore his eyes away to look at Luke. "Luke, man, where are you hurt?" he asked, not liking how pale his friend was. Luke turned glazed eyes towards Landon and seemed to be struggling with his reply. In the end though, he couldn't find the strength and Landon watched as Luke's eyes rolled a little before shutting, his body slumping a little to the side. "Luke!" he screamed, finally spotting the blood seeping through the vest and he moved to stem the blood flow with the bandages Adrian tossed his way.

"Let's load them up!" Jeremiah said, taking control of the situation. "The sooner we're back on base, the better. Hurry now."

Carefully, everyone was moved over to the other truck, the first truck too damaged to be of further use at the moment, and then those who were still okay hung on as the truck roared its way back to base, careful to keep the pressure on their friends' wounds all the while.

Majors Brunner and Leahy ran up as it stopped just outside the designated aircraft area. "What happened? We heard the explosions and gunfire from here!"

Landon barely heard Jeremiah's answer concerning something about a small, likely isolated incident with some of the local rebels as he carried Luke over to the helicopter with Frank's help, not even waiting for the order to do so. As soon as he'd settled Luke down, he saw Adrian and Dwayne carry Hudson over as well. Again, Landon met Adrian's eyes, worry clearly written on both friends' faces.

It wasn't soon enough for either of them when they were back up in the air speeding their way back to the medic base.

8

A siren blared, bringing Jamie's head snapping up from the late lunch she had just sat down to have, her morning rounds having run grossly overtime.

"All available medical personnel," a voice sounded over the speaker system. "Please report to surgery. Incoming wounded in twenty minutes."

With a sigh, Jamie stuffed her mouth with some food before she stood up and carried her tray over to the garbage can to throw the rest away.

"Some lunch, huh?" an aide asked as she joined Jamie for the short walk over to the temp building that served as the surgery area to start prepping.

"A mouthful is better than nothing at all. I remember a time during residency when I was able to get that much in a day or more. At least I was able to get breakfast this morning."

"That busy of a base?"

Jamie nodded. "And being here, it seems like I'm doing my residency all over again only this time, the only one grading me is myself."

"It must be a lot of pressure knowing that when lives hang on the balance, you have the ability to determine life or death for these people."

She gave a shrug. "I do what I can and hope it's enough. The rest is up to the patient."

The other woman nodded her head in agreement

as the two entered the building. Jamie waved bye to the other woman as she made her way to the right to scrub in at the sink.

"Good, you're here. Dr. Scott, you'll be at station two. I have Devin and Janine helping you out there."

"Sounds good, sir. What's the case history?"

"Your soldier is a twenty-four year old male, name Louis Moreno. Sounds like his truck got hit with an IED just about an hour ago."

"So I've got burns and foreign body removal to look out for, great!" she said in a cheery voice before sobering. "It never ends, does it?"

Dr. Taff gave her a sympathetic smile. "Chin up, Jamie," he said as he took his turn at the sink. "It'll be over soon enough."

"You're scrubbing in too?"

"The incoming helicopter has plenty of wounded needing attention today, your patient wasn't alone. Besides us, I've called in Drs. Fong, Olsen, and Gross as well."

"It'll be nice and cozy in surgery that's for sure," she smiled as she headed into the next room where the energy level was already high as everyone got ready.

Jamie walked over to the second table and smiled. "Devin, Janine, are we all set?"

"Yes, doctor," came the reply from the Asian woman across the table from her.

"Good. Were we able to pull up any stats on Moreno?"

"Right here," replied Devin as he held up a few sheets and flipped through them for her, the papers listing the patient's basic health history and vitals records.

A quick scan showed Jamie nothing remarkable enough to pique her interest. "Good, nothing to worry about except said injuries," she muttered to herself as the noise of an approaching helicopter began to reach their ears.

She turned to the doctor at the table next to her and caught him saying a couple of things to his team. "...blood loss, which has been pre-determined to be from a couple of wounds to the back, but not entirely positive since there's also report of a wound on his chest too."

"Maybe a bullet went straight through him?"

"Can't rule it out, so I need you to monitor Mr. Thompson's situation critically. He's already lost a lot of blood and we don't want him to lose anymore, understood?" Dr. Fong turned around then only to find Jamie staring back at him. "Dr. Scott? Are you all right?"

She ignored the question to ask one of her own. "Your patient's not a Luke Thompson, is it?"

"Yes, why? Jamie!" He called after her as she just rushed out the door.

She found Dr. Taff just outside the door giving a few last instructions to a couple of other people. As soon as he'd dismissed them, Jamie stepped up to the man, causing him to take an involuntary step back. "Who else is coming in?"

He looked at her in surprise. "I told you. I paged for Dr. Fong and Dr.-"

"No, that's not what I meant. The patients."

He continued to give her a strange look. "I

assigned Dr. Fong to a Luke Thompson, Dr. Olsen to Robin Johnston, I'm working on Hudson Nelson, and Dr. Gross is going to start assessing the non-critical patients. Jamie, what's wrong?"

"My husband, Landon Scott, was he hurt? Or his friend Adrian Roberts? Luke and Hudson are close friends of theirs and they were all out on the same excursion just now, so if they're hurt…"

A pained look had settled onto Jamie's face as she anxiously awaited the words that would come out of Dr. Taff's mouth next and understanding settled onto the man's features a he quickly recalled the list that had been radioed ahead to him and he shook his head no. "Jamie, are you going to be okay in there? I can reassign Dr. Gross to take your place and you can work with the non-criticals," he offered.

She shook her head. "Too late," she said as they heard the helicopter land and the cargo door slide open. "I'll be okay," she added, seeing the unconvinced look on her supervisor's face. "My patient will be depending on me."

He continued to look grim but nodded in the end. "Look Jamie, I gave you Moreno because I trust you to try and work some of that magic of yours on him. He'll need it, but if you need to switch…"

She shook her head as she started to head back into the surgery room and he followed. "I'll be fine. Just do your best for Hudson." She saw Dr. Fong give her a questioning look as she moved back to the second table and she tried to give a reassuring smile before donning on a face mask. It seemed to work because he didn't say anything further to her, both their attentions shifting to the door as the first patient was brought in.

"Nelson?" a voice called.

Jamie watched as Adrian and another soldier carried Hudson in their arms over to the third table, which was diagonally across from hers, as directed.

"Thompson?"

Landon's voice sent Jamie's heart racing into overdrive as he helped carry Luke to the table across the way from her.

'And so this war finally hits close to home,' she thought as she briefly caught both their gazes, a shared kind of terror in all their eyes as they thought of the implications.

"Moreno?"

Jamie snapped out of it long enough to call out to the latest pair of soldiers and direct them over. She shot one last look at her friends and nodded before she turned to her patient, calling on every ounce of strength she had to be the doctor she'd trained to be.

"Mr. Moreno? Mr. Moreno, can you hear me?" she asked loudly in her patient's ear in hopes of getting any type of response as she held onto one wrist to check the pulse. Devin and Janine were already working on cutting away and discarding the scorched clothing from the body to allow Jamie a better look at what she was up against. She hid her grimace as she saw the burns and squeezed the patient's bloody hand. "All right, Mr. Moreno. It looks like we're going to have you here for awhile. I want you to hang on for me, okay? Just hang on and we'll get you fixed up here," she announced to the still non-responsive body before her.

Jamie took one last look over at where Luke and Hudson were laying, said a silent prayer, and finally turned to her two aides. "All right. Let's get this show on the road."

9

Hours passed and still Jamie worked on trying to piece her patient back together as best she could. After a cursory wipe down to get rid of some of the dirt and dried blood, Jamie had painstakingly worked to flush wounds clean and stitch them shut, an arduous task considering the extent of his injuries resulting from his proximity to the explosion.

"How's he doing?" she asked as she worked on finally addressing the last of his less critical wounds, this one a jagged gash that crept from his shoulder down his right arm that got deep and close to bone in some areas.

"Heart rate's still steady, blood pressure and oxygen levels also still normal."

"Looks like you're going to make it, Mr. Moreno, you're doing great," she smiled as she continued a one-sided conversation with her unconscious patient, a habit she never got over from her days as a student. "Just a few more bandages and you'll be good to go."

With one last snip, she cut off the ends of the surgical thread and beckoned for Devin to start bandaging up the arm, mentally giving thanks that there were no broken bones to try to set here. She herself took a small step away and rolled her head and shoulders around to relieve the tension she felt there. She then turned and glanced around the room to see Drs. Fong and Olsen still huddled over their patients working steadily away. The third station sat empty. 'Dr. Taff's good but that quick? Oh God, Hudson!' An icy feeling settled inside her and the feeling of dread suddenly threatened to overwhelm her as she forced herself to think of the reality of the situation in front of her.

Mumbling some kind of excuse and letting Janine know she'd have her pager on in case they needed her back, she found herself walking out of the room in a sudden desperate need for fresh air. She tore off her bloodied scrubs and mask out by a sink and rinsed her face, trying to will her tears to keep from flowing. "Come on, Jamie. If there are miracle workers out there, you know Dr. Taff is one of them. You can't be sure about Hudson, he could be all right."

After drying off, she stepped outside only to find both Landon and Adrian outside waiting. In the dying sunlight, she could see the redness in Landon's eyes and her heart plummeted. Quickly, she grasped his hand and felt his trembling. When he spotted her, she watched as Adrian struggled to find words to say, his mouth opening and closing, ineffectively making any sound except for a choked cry that stripped away yet more of Jamie's strength. The helpless look on his face made him look younger than he was, and the tears that had begun to course down Landon's face again were all Jamie needed to let loose a few of her own tears.

Landon clung to his wife and she held him close, trying to lend him some of her strength as he cried openly. The helpless and lost look on Adrian's face tore her up and so she beckoned to him as well, Jamie comforting both men as best she could, her family in this hell they were living in.

"Come on, let's go to the dining commons. I need to eat and we can wait there to get the news on Luke. Dr. Fong is still working on him," she suggested as she directed the two away from the surgery building. "Have you eaten yet?"

Landon took in a shaky breath and shook his head, trying to gain control of his emotions before responding. "We couldn't leave, not without word."

"We didn't even think about it," Adrian added.

She gave him a comforting pat on the arm with one hand, her other arm wrapped around Landon's waist as they continued to walk. "Well starving yourselves isn't going to help so we might as well get you fed. It'll help, I think."

The boys nodded as they each grabbed a tray and grabbed some of the remaining food that had been left out after the main dining hours were complete. Once settled down at one table, they began to eat in silence, each one lost in their own thoughts.

Some minutes passed before Adrian was able to ask the question he'd been wanting to have answered since he'd seen her step out of surgery. "Jamie, did you know?"

Jamie looked up at the man across the table from her. 'He looks so young and vulnerable, no wonder the girls loved him back then and honestly, probably still do. And yet, all the stress and worry has added years to his face and body. War ages a person in so many ways,' she thought as she noted the worn expression on his face. "Know what?"

"When he... when he..."

Adrian couldn't find the strength to say the word just yet so she did it for him. "Died?" she finished quietly. Tears threatened to spill over onto his face, but he just nodded his head and tried to blink them away. She shook her head sadly. "No, I didn't," she answered honestly and quietly. "I had my own patient to worry about. What happened to Hudson, if you don't mind me asking."

Adrian gave a sigh. "From what one of the guys said in that truck, besides the driver, he got the biggest hit from the IED. No amount of protection gear could have helped out more than what he already had on. He'd lost a lot of blood by the time we even reached him, and adding the extra time it took for us to get him here..." His voice faltered and Jamie watched as the tears begin slipping down Adrian's face anew. "I tried to help, Jamie, I really did. But there was just so much blood. It was so much..."

With a look to Landon and one last squeeze of his hand, Jamie stood up and took the seat next to their friend, taking him into her arms. "Shh, there now, Adrian. I know you tried your best. It's okay now, really. It'll be okay," she tried to comfort the boy – 'man,' she corrected in her head, recognizing that he was moving through the shock of losing a friend and brother. Landon was shooting her a look though that asked her an unspoken question, and she sighed a little even as she continued to hold onto Adrian as he cried. 'It's true. Will any of us be truly okay after all of this is said and done?'

- - -

Night had fallen and she had finally convinced the guys to give in to their exhaustion and get some rest. Letting them know that keeping vigil at Luke's bed in the recovery room wouldn't help the situation didn't go over so well, but once she'd given them a promise that someone would let them know as soon as possible if anything changed in Luke's situation, the guys had given in and she led them to their building and their beds for some much needed sleep.

As for her, well... 'It's probably best if I were asleep now too rather than running,' she thought even as her feet pounded evenly on the ground as she pushed herself to make another circuit around inside their walled encampment. Part of her need came from still being on a little bit of an adrenaline rush after surgery. The larger drive though was her need to think, to get her thoughts and feelings sorted through before they could plague her dreams at night.

'As if my dreams weren't already haunted by the what if's and could have been's,' she thought.

She encountered few people on her run. Most everyone was asleep, but there were a few other off duty soldiers like her who were taking advantage of the cool night air to do other things.

'So we've finally lost our first. Perhaps it was too much to ask for all of us to make it out of here untouched. Would I have wanted it any other way though? Of course I didn't want any of them to die, but it still doesn't change the fact that Hudson is gone and things will never be the same again.

'And yet, that's life, isn't it? Things always change. Life happens, bringing with it the good and the bad. It's how we move through it and embrace it all that's important. And here especially, we don't have the luxury of being able to stop every time something awful happens and figure out the possible consequences of this or that action. We react and move on... It could just as easily have been Landon's truck that got hit or Adrian getting shot at, but it wasn't.

'Is it so wrong though that I feel a little relieved that things turned out the way they did? That I'm spared the brunt of the pain of losing someone that close to me even though I know Hudson's family will be devastated by the news? Yes, I think Hudson and Luke are like older brothers and Adrian the younger brother I never had, but it's not the same for me. I've only known the guys now a few years. These guys have known each other for more than half their lives. In their eyes, losing Hudson *is* losing family. This is going to be a hard one for them all to get over, and I suspect especially for Adrian since he was the one trying to help out the most there in the end.'

Jamie thought of the small pile of letters with Hudson's handwriting on them sitting in her desk next to her waiting bed and gave a little sigh as she began her cool down a little while later. 'Those will have to go out first thing in the morning. I'll have to ask Dr. Taff too if someone has reached his family in the meantime. If he hasn't gotten to it yet, it might help if I were the one to make that call.

'But what about Luke though and his family,' she wondered as she found herself being drawn into the recovery room. With the aid of only the moonlight filtering in through the windows, she made her way over to Luke's bed and took a seat in the chair next to it. She took one cool hand into hers and watched silently for a little while as he lay there, listening to his shallow but steady breathing. She thought back to dinner when a soldier had approached the three of them and asked how Hudson and Luke were doing. When he'd heard, his face had fallen, but he did tell his side of the story, saying how Luke had pushed him down and over when he had spotted someone coming out of the trees and shot the guy. Unfortunately for Luke though, he hadn't seen another guy coming in from another direction before getting shot at.

"We didn't think it was a big deal at first," the man, Dwayne, had said. "He just turned around and shot back, killing the other guy before he could get any closer. But then as soon as the firing had stopped, I noticed that his breathing had gotten all raspy and he was getting a little pale. Next thing I knew, he was unconscious."

"You had to play the hero, didn't you, Luke?" Jamie found herself asking quietly, mindful of the other sleeping injured individuals nearby. "Living up to your dream and being a true Superman. He's alive thanks to you, you know. You should be proud of yourself. Not many people out there would have acted as selflessly, ensuring that others around are all safe first. You did good, Luke. You did good."

She squeezed Luke's hand a little bit and felt her

breath catch when she felt an almost imperceptible bit of pressure squeeze back on her hand. Then she listened as Luke's breathing slowed even further and faltered. In the time it took for Jamie to jump out of her seat, and reach for one of the alarms to page another of the attendings to help her get the necessary equipment over to Luke's bed, his breathing had stopped completely. No amount of resuscitation could bring the man back, and it wasn't too long before Jamie was left alone again with the body of what had once been her friend. She took a hand in hers again, feeling as the warmth of the body steadily left and allowed a few more tears to slip down from her eyes, her gaze never leaving the ghostly smile that still played on Luke's lips.

10

A month had passed since Hudson and Luke had died and it had been as hard on the guys as Jamie had expected. Landon was more quiet than normal, his mood more thoughtful when he wasn't out on active patrol or duty. Jamie often caught him glancing her way when they were together, and each time he did, her automatic response had been to smile back in reassurance.

Still, if she worried about Landon, she had been even more worried with Adrian. As she had anticipated, the other blonde male had taken the deaths hard, Hudson's especially, even going so far as to blame himself in some way. Between the shock and the blame, Jamie had noticed that Adrian just didn't smile nearly as often now and there had been almost a permanent kind of cloud that hung around the once lively and energetic youngster of the group those first couple of weeks. 'God, it breaks my heart just thinking about what those two have gone through already. They're too young to have gone through so much pain…'

It had been hard for the guys coming back to a half empty room. After being too exhausted and too emotionally drained to think about it the night of the attack, the reality had hit when they had awakened to a light knocking on the door the next morning. Jamie had been there, the bearer of more bad news as she told them of Luke's passing during the night. Before the guys could get upset at not being told earlier, she let them know that it had been sudden but that she had been there personally.

"He wouldn't have wanted to wake you guys for nothing, you know," she had told them. "If it helps any, he died peacefully…"

She had helped the guys pack up their friends' belongings to send back to the states along with the letters that each had written over the time they'd been away and which had, up to that point, been in Jamie's care.

Another couple of days had passed before two other guys moved in to occupy the empty beds in the small quarters that Landon and Adrian still shared. "And a mixed kind of blessing that has been," Jamie muttered to herself. "The guys don't have to be haunted by sights of empty beds whenever they get back, but it doesn't help either that the guys who are in those beds aren't Hudson or Luke. Still, at least they're good, nice guys and their company is helping when I can't be around them…"

She slowed her jog around the inside barriers of the compound to a walk, taking in a deep breath of the fresh night air to refresh her. Tonight's run had led her to stop in front of Landon's sleeping quarters again. The lights inside had been long since turned off for the night and she made no attempt to disturb the guys as they slept. Instead, she found herself taking a seat next to the door and leaned back against the wall to rest, waiting for her heart to calm all the way down. As she sat there, she looked up into the skies above her and found herself sending a prayer up to the heavens. "Please, God, watch over these men inside for me. The fighting has been escalating outside these compound walls, causing the guys to be gone more and more often, risking their lives every day they're off base. And while part of me is glad that they're keeping busy, I can't help but worry. Each time they leave, I can't help but wonder if they'll make it back safe and sound. All that fighting means I'm kept in the ward for longer periods, and I never know if I'll see them before they head out anymore. I'm just worried about them. They're still mourning from the loss of their friends, and while they're getting better and no longer in that deep state of shock as they had been those first few days, I feel like they're going out distracted and not entirely there, and they need all their wits about them to concentrate in battle. Please, God, just watch over these men for me. I don't know if I could be of anymore use out here if we were to lose another…"

- - -

The sirens were blaring again at the compound as Jamie rushed out of her sleeping quarters, giving her a small sense of déjà vu. The circumstances were different now though. Rather than expecting helicopters of injured people to arrive at any minute, the sirens were instead signaling the compound's imminent desertion. The attacks around the compound had grown increasingly worse and the powers that be had decided that rather than risk a direct attack on the compound, it would be safer for everyone to move out to another strategic location a couple hours away by air.

For Jamie, it was too far, if only because there was a nagging voice in her mind telling her that Landon and Adrian wouldn't know where they had gone. Their troop had left the compound a week ago for another extended excursion and had been scheduled to come back today.

"You'll be one of the first to know if something happens out there with them, trust us," Jamie had recalled one director saying to her during one of her rare breaks earlier on in the week. "For now, just think that no news is good news."

'No news may be good news, but what about today? Will they hold a transport here for them when they come back?' she asked herself as she finished stuffing her pack and ran out to one of the waiting helicopters, her eyes quickly scanning to see if the guys had arrived yet sometime during all the hectic packing. Swallowing a sigh when she saw her hopes were in vain, she threw her pack aboard to one of the crew members before heading back towards the ward to quickly help finish prepping the injured for travel.

"Dr. Scott! Patient 1!"

She rushed over to where Dr. Fong and a couple of medical assistants were waiting for a fourth person to help carry the patient over to the helicopter carrier. As soon as she had grabbed the last corner of the sheets that would serve as the means of transport, Dr. Fong unplugged the last few cords connecting the man to the bed, laid the loose ends on the man's body, and they were off and rushing as best they could. At the helicopter, Dr. Taff and Dr. Gross were waiting to receive the patient and immediately hook him up to the monitoring equipment already on board.

The routine continued a few times more and then they were soon up and lifting off into the air, one of the last helicopters lifting up out of the compound, the blaring of the sirens slowly being drowned out by the drone of the helicopter's blades and the whirring of all the medical equipment inside as well. Jamie's quick eyes searched the compound, taking inventory and going through her mental list again to make sure everything that could have been done was done. It was as they were slowly climbing up into the air though that Jamie's eyes quick eyes saw bursts of light coming from their right, near the compound gates. As they rose, she caught glimpses of hostile faces and could just make out the faint bursts of gunfire above the wailing sirens and helicopter drone. "Talk about leaving just in time," she vaguely heard Devin saying behind her.

She rushed to close the hatch door as the others took care of the patients but found her heart rate speeding up even more as she looked past the gate and spotted a caravan of trucks from their own side making their way towards the compound. Her heart leapt up to her throat and she found herself sinking onto the helicopter floor, unable to find the strength to close it now as she watched in horror as the gunmen turned their attention to the oncoming vehicles.

"NO!" she screamed at the top of her lungs as

gunfire erupted again and she saw the front truck swerve. Somehow, it managed to stay on the road and continued to barrel forward, but before she could make it out anymore, she felt a solid pair of arms grab her around the waist and drag her away from the door.

"What are you doing?" Dr. Fong was yelling at her, trying to be heard over the noise.

As soon as he had managed to shut the door, Dr. Gross turned back to where Dr. Fong was trying to restrain Jamie. "Are you hurt? Where were you hit?" he asked, checking Jamie quickly for any surface wounds and finding none visible.

Jamie shook her head as she tried to wrestle herself out of his grasp, her need to rush towards another window overwhelming her. "No, no, not me. We have to go back! Landon and the guys are here, and they're driving straight into that ambush! We have to go back and help!"

The other two doctors glanced quickly at each other worriedly. "That's not our position! We're out! They're going to have to catch the next transport!" Dr. Fong yelled above the drone of the machinery around them, trying to explain. He almost regretted his words though as she struggled that much harder in his grasp and he found himself having to grip tighter to maintain his hold around her.

Dr. Gross crouched in front of them. "Jamie!" When she continued to struggle, he gave a quick snap in front of her eyes. "Dr. Scott!" Her eyes slowly focused on the worried brown eyes of the doctor in front of her. When he was sure he had more of her attention, he continued on in a gentler tone. "We need you here, right now, 100% Jamie. Stay with me. Those guys on the ground, they know what to do and the convoy will get word about where to go from there. There's nothing else that we can do right now but take care of the patients we have here. They need you. Can you do that for me?"

Jamie looked into the concerned brown eyes and fought to control her panic. She eventually found herself closing her eyes and giving a sigh. With a nod of her head, she felt Dr. Fong ease up on his grip around her and she took a few more moments to collect herself before opening her eyes once again, but not before she sent out another silent prayer asking for the safety of the man she loved.

11

"All right, tell me again why we're doing this?" Adrian asked as he and Landon made their way in the pouring rain through some dense forest on a trek to some ruins.

"Do you want the official reason or just my educated guess?" Landon asked as the grumble of thunder echoed around them. His rifle was clutched tightly in his hands, his eyes trying to scan the green and brown world around them for any sign of enemy presence.

"Seriously, whatever intelligence our superiors are getting seems more wrong than right. I feel like we're just on some wild goose chase."

"Would you rather be in combat? Sure it seems like we've just been doing busy foot work, trekking through this mud and all, but I still think it's better than being caught in crossfire."

"You do have a point there," he admitted, his blue eyes squinting against the rain. "But at the same time, I don't know. You've heard the talk. There's definitely more fighting going on around here these days and it seems to be getting closer and closer to base. We're going to be caught up in some bad action sooner rather than later I think."

Landon sighed to himself and stayed quiet. The exact same thoughts had passed through his head as well and he had no reason to argue such thinking but... 'That doesn't mean I can't keep from hoping or praying that something like that won't happen,' he thought as they approached a small pile of rubble that used to have been part of the abandoned excavation site they were now entering.

Adrian and Landon both instinctively slowed their pace, taking more care now to note their surroundings for any human signs as the forest around them thinned a little bit.

They carefully combed the area, slowly drawing closer to the larger temple they could just see through the thinning greenery. Off in the distance opposite them, they spotted another pair of soldiers coming closer from the other direction. A quick glance through a pair of binoculars showed Adrian that the soldiers were their own so he signaled to Landon to keep moving on. Before putting the binoculars away, he took a glance eastward and found another pair of fellow soldiers moving in from that direction. The trees blocked his view to the west and so he finally put the binoculars away and re-shouldered his rifle.

"We've got two other pairs moving in, one from the south and one from the east," Adrian said quietly to his partner, joining Landon at another stone mound.

"Where are Manuel and Caden?" Landon asked out loud, a sense of unease growing in his gut.

"I couldn't see behind the trees or the temple, but I'm assuming they're almost here too. The guys in the east didn't indicate anything was wrong."

"And I don't like having to make assumptions," Landon muttered to himself under his breath. He spotted the mound first a few moments later and moved towards it, crouching down to take a closer look. "Well lookie here..."

Adrian glanced over to see Landon veering away from him and he followed suit. "What is it?"

"I don't know, but whatever it is, it doesn't belong here," he replied as he used his rifle to brush off some of the leaves and dirt off it to reveal a small pile of scrap metal.

"Unless the ancient people who lived here ages ago knew about metal working," Adrian added.

"It could have been left by the excavators but somehow, I highly doubt that. There's no rust," he said, giving Adrian a grim look.

"It's recent," Adrian replied, understanding in his eyes.

At the bottom of the pile, underneath some larger pieces of scrap metal, Landon spotted the pile of guns and ammunition and he glanced back over to Adrian. "Looks like someone's been here all right. You better radio back to the jeep." He paused long enough for Adrian to ID himself on the earpiece he wore and give the situation before describing the pile and hearing Adrian echo him. "We've got a small pile of munitions here, some fifteen to twenty old and worn semi-automatic pistols, maybe a hundred cases of bullets..."

Landon paused as he spotted something at the very bottom of the pile flash a red light. Pushing aside a couple of small cases out of the way, he saw red numbers counting down... "6...5...4..."

"It's a trap!" Landon shouted as he scrambled up from his position and shoved Adrian violently away from the metal scrap heap.

Before they'd taken two steps, there was an explosion from the west and the two heard immediate screaming follow.

"Mayday, mayday!" Adrian screamed into his microphone. "It was a trap! The place is boobytrapped with explosives and the west team is down. We need backup!"

His comment was interrupted by explosions from the south and from the pile they had just left a few feet behind them, the power of the blasts enough to cause them to stumble to the ground though thankfully, little of the shrapnel got directed toward them. Even as the two scrambled back to their feet though, Landon risked a glance towards the temple and felt his heart sink as he saw shadowed figures detaching themselves from the worn stones and temple recesses. He half listened as Adrian continued to describe the turn of events into his headpiece and both of them tried to dodge the spray of bullets now aiming straight for them.

"We are under attack!" Adrian screamed. "I repeat, we are under attack! Come get us out of here!"

'God, please, just get us out of here,' Landon echoed in his head as they tried to reach the cover of the forest. It was hard going though with the rain now steadily coming down and their feet sinking in the muddy terrain with each step. He felt a sharp sting on his left arm and knew he'd been grazed by a bullet but didn't even bother to spare a glance down at it in his need to get away. He turned slightly to fire a few rounds behind him before he pushed on, following Adrian.

"Five minutes!?" he heard him scream. "We need out of here now!" The taller blonde barely suppressed a curse as a couple of bullets grazed one of his arms too. "Look, we're going to try to get back to the drop off point. Make sure you're there by the time we are!"

It seemed like forever before the two of them realized that the forest was once again silent all around them, the gunfire no longer an immediate threat to their lives for the moment. The silence was not wholly reassuring however, and they hurried along as best they could anyway, guns firmly in hand just in case.

"Manuel? Ethan? Raymond? Any of you guys okay? Anyone of you hear me?" Adrian asked, pressing the earpiece closer, trying to catch any sound on the other end. "Manuel? Ethan? Raymond? It's Adrian. Can you hear me?"

Landon glanced over as they both waited for any sort of answer. When none came, he just shook his head and forced himself to press on. Adrian tried once more, calling out to the guys, but only an empty silence answered in return.

They continued on silently for a tense few moments, each using the time to gather their swirling thoughts together. Every few steps, Landon would glance at his wrist to check the compass to make sure they were still headed in the right direction, but besides that communication, all else was silent.

The taller blonde was the first to break the silence. "You know, that has got to be the closest we've come to getting hit yet."

Landon had to agree. "I know, but it seems as if someone's looking out for us," he replied, pointing upwards to the sky. "And that means we're not done here."

Adrian gave a small smile. "Well said. I think you've been around Jamie too much. You've gone all optimistic on me."

"That's a laugh. We've both been hanging around her, and your personality hasn't changed."

"Well, you are supposed to be the brooding bass of the group," he remarked with a touch of sarcasm lacing his words.

"I think I prefer 'thoughtful'."

This time, Adrian let out a dry chuckle. "All right, oh thoughtful one. Do you have any other pearls of wisdom to spout?"

Landon was about to reply when a low rumbling caught his ear. After getting used to the muted sounds of the rain coming down through the trees, it was only another short moment before Adrian heard it too, a low humming in discord with the natural sounds around them, and he slowed down to match Landon's cautious pace. Landon glanced at his wrist again. "It's coming from the right place," he said lowly.

Just then, Adrian heard a familiar voice coming through his earpiece. "Rover One, Rover One here."

A smile crossed his face. "Well I'm glad someone's coming. Have I told you what a beautiful voice you have, Kaylee?" he asked as he picked up the pace and Landon followed suit.

"Oh stop the sweet talk already, honey, or I'll

have to tell your sweetie Katie on you."

He chuckled. "Now that's an empty threat if there ever was one," he replied back just as the Jeep pulled into view still some yards away.

Landon gave a sigh of relief as he raised an arm in greeting at Kaylee as she drove closer. Just then, the sharp sound they immediately recognized as gunfire came from behind them. Quickly, Landon and Adrian crouched lower as they began running full out and an onslaught of bullets were fired their way. "Kaylee, keep down and stay where you're at. We'll get to you," Adrian urged.

"Y'all stop playing martyr now. I see you guys – just give me two more seconds," all trace of joking gone from her voice to be replaced with a steely tone to it instead.

Adrian winced as he felt a fresh sting brush his arm close to the first ones he'd gotten just minutes before and just managed to bite back a curse. 'We may not have another two seconds,' he thought as he pushed himself to go faster. Just then, he grunted as he felt a sudden burst of pain shoot up from his right leg. Without thinking twice about it, he immediately spun around and fired back a few rounds of shots, satisfied when it seemed the gunfire faltered for a moment.

"Adrian, what are you doing!?"

"Keep going, Landon, and get in that Jeep. No need to go break Jamie's heart," was the reply he gave as he continued to shoot in the direction they'd just come from.

Landon's green eyes watched as the Jeep came even closer, but found himself turning back to get

Adrian. With a firm grip to his friend's shoulders, he attempted to drag Adrian up to his feet. "As if I'd let Katie experience heartache if I could help it."

Adrian felt his weight give out on his right side though and this time, he could not keep the low groan from escaping. "Shit, Landon. Just go already."

Landon was only beginning to comprehend that Adrian had been hurt when the door to the Jeep flung wide open as it pulled up. Snapping himself out of it, he almost found himself snapping back. "Not without my brother," he almost growled as he and another soldier hoisted Adrian up into the vehicle. As soon as they were both in, the Jeep lurched forward. Gunfire continued to erupt, and for awhile, it seemed like they were all making their mark on the Jeep as it plowed on. It lasted only a few moments though, and soon the sounds of gunfire had disappeared altogether once more.

"Y'all okay back there?" Kaylee asked as she glanced back in the rearview mirror.

"Thankful you came when you did is all," Landon managed before turning back to Adrian. "All right, where were you hit?" He was already digging through his opened pack for his first aid supplies.

"Leg," he gritted, his hands holding the back of his right calf tightly, trying to maintain pressure.

Landon drew out a few scraps of cloth and bent to wrap them above the wound to stem the flow of blood escaping through the wound.

The other man in the Jeep with them finished cutting away Adrian's pants to let them see the damage, and as soon as that was cleared away, he got to work cleaning the wounds with alcohol.

"Rover One to base, Rover One to base, we have the north team back safely, one wounded, no word from the others," Kaylee said into the intercom on the dashboard.

"Copy that Rover One. Any chance you'd be able to get to that temple to check on and perhaps get the others?" another voice asked.

"Base, this is Adrian of the north team. I've been trying to get in contact with the other teams since we were attacked and have gotten no response. The site was heavily guarded with enough bodies to even trail Landon and I back to our rendezvous spot. If we go back, we'd need to do so with more equipment and bodies," he managed to get out, trying his best to keep the pain out of his voice.

"Copy that north team. Rover One, head over to the post forty-five miles south of where you are and meet Rovers Two and Four. The coordinates are on your screen now. When you're all together, head back to base."

"Copy that," Kaylee replied before glancing back in the rearview mirror. "How are you boys doing in the back?"

Adrian couldn't help but hiss as the alcohol burned his skin nor could he help the tears that spilled from his eyes. His hands gripped onto the side of the Jeep as tight as he could, trying to ignore the pain radiating up from his leg. "As well as can be," he managed.

Landon freed Adrian's foot from his boot. "All right man, can you wiggle your toes for me? Can you feel me touching your foot here?" He gave a small sigh of relief when Adrian demonstrated that there was no nerve damage, and then found himself giving a small chuckle. At the curious looks he received, he explained himself, "Sorry, but I was just thinking that of course you'd find a way to get yourself out of combat sooner rather than later."

Adrian managed to roll his eyes before taking the pain pills the dark-haired man to his right were offering, nodding his thanks. "Right, because getting shot was the number one item on my list of things to do today. Can I just say, so not worth it?"

Kaylee laughed from the driver seat up front, her gleaming teeth a contrast to her dark, mocha skin. "Keep up that sense of humor there, Adrian, dear. You'll be getting some proper care soon."

"Yeah, within an hour with the way you drive," Adrian joked back weakly, his adrenaline rush fading, before completely laying back on the floor of the modified Jeep, all seats removed besides the driver's seat.

"What can I say? I'm a girl who likes it fast. Y'all just hang on and enjoy the ride."

It took them closer to an hour and a half just to reach the site where two other Jeeps were already waiting, the rain and mud having made the going slower than anticipated. Without waiting for their Jeep to stop, the other two vehicles turned and started driving off, Kaylee falling in line behind the other two Jeeps.

"Almost there. You holding up, Adrian?"

"For now perhaps, but the sooner we get to base, the sooner we'll have the proper instruments to chop this leg off," he answered Kaylee from where he was laying on the floor, his leg propped up against one of their bags to help minimize the bleeding.

"That bad, huh?" Landon asked, trying hard to keep his voice light and keep all the worry out of it. Inside though, his heart was pounding as he watched his friend steadily albeit slowly continue to lose blood. "Can you still wiggle your toes?" When Adrian complied, Landon grinned. "No chopping today. Besides, I think Jamie's partial to having her friends stay whole if they can help it. No need to go disappointing her now."

The caravan of three Jeeps thundered along as quickly as they could and Landon tried his best not to count the minutes that passed as they headed closer to base. Soon enough, they were on a more worn out path and the surroundings became more and more familiar, giving Landon cause to smile. 'We're almost there…'

Just as they rounded the last bend that led directly to the front gates, however, the sharp static of gunfire reached the ears of everyone on board, even through the drone of the helicopters that were lifting off into the air.

"Out of one battle and into another?" Adrian asked, unable to see much of the outside world from his vantage point.

Landon gave a tight nod. "I know that things were getting bad close to base but didn't realize it was this bad." Suddenly, he paled. "Jamie…"

"Helicopters are leaving as we speak. She could be on any one of them so don't you even worry about her. Let's just get ourselves past these guns,"

Kaylee said, trying to soothe the man. Just then, she noticed the front Jeep swerve towards the left suddenly, though somehow, it managed to stay upright. "Oh shit," she said under her breath.

"Looks like they've noticed us coming in," the other man in their Jeep said, tightness forming around his eyes and his mouth. Without a word, he picked up his rifle and quickly checked to make sure everything looked clear before scooting closer to his window.

Landon followed suit, buckling his helmet back on tight first and making sure he had fresh rounds within easy reach after muttering a quick prayer under his breath. Soon, he too was cautiously peering out of the window on his side of the vehicle.

"Rovers, this is Rover Two. We're going in. Cover us, will you?" a male voice came over the intercom on the dashboard.

"This is Rover One. We're covering your tails, go ahead," Kaylee replied, keeping close to the vehicles in front of her.

The scenery continued to fly by at a rapid pace, the stretch to the gates already a long one. For Adrian, however, that path seemed to go so much longer from his vantage point on the floor. He watched as Landon clicked down the telescope on his rifle but didn't look through it just yet, wanting to keep as wide a field of view as possible for now as he scanned the areas around the front gate for a clue as to where the shots were being fired from. The man to Adrian's right was humming a little tune under his breath as his cool eyes also searched the surrounding areas for a clean shot. And Kaylee was doing her best to keep them upright, especially as the Jeep at the front of their caravan swerved again just as it got within a couple hundred feet of the main gates. Again, somehow, it continued to barrel on, and just a few moments later, it was their turn to rumble through the gates. By then though, the gunfire had stopped completely.

"What are they waiting for?" someone's voice came across the intercom, the air eerily silent except for the rumble of the caravan.

"Maybe they got scared off when reinforcements arrived," another voice replied.

Adrian gave a soft scoff. "I heard copters taking off. Either the big game they were after is gone or…"

He trailed off, not wanting to finish his sentence, but Landon finished for him anyway. "Or we're being corralled in."

Even as those thoughts threatened to sink the spirit of the convoy even more, a commanding voice came across the intercom. "Rovers, glad you made it. Transfer over to the helipad – you guys are the last ones out. Everything's been loaded. Just move. Further instructions will be transmitted on board once you are clear of the area."

There was something haunting about the compound with it being empty save for the two helicopters they approached, engines already whirring as the convoy had began their approach. Their vehicles had just stopped when the group finally heard something unexpected. The air echoed with what sounded like a legion of hellions descending upon them, and the sharp sound of gunfire started a fresh round at the same time.

"Left side, boys!" Kaylee shouted to her passengers, glad they had parked in a way that shielded their route towards the copters as best as possible.

"Silly thing to ask if you can put any pressure at all on your leg, huh?" Landon asked even as he exited the car and turned to give Adrian a shoulder to lean on.

Kaylee flanked Adrian and Landon as the two made their way the few feet between the jeep and copter, Landon doing more to carry his taller friend than Adrian could unfortunately help. The seconds slipped by agonizingly slow, however, and everyone knew that their next step could be the last. Somehow their group managed to get to one helicopter safely, its blades turning, almost ready for takeoff. Once Adrian had been taken up into the copter's belly though, being helped up by the fourth man of their team, Landon turned to Kaylee and gave her a boost up. She had just made it up and was turning to give Landon a hand as well when the first rebel fighter finally came rounding the base walls and began firing their way in earnest even as other rebels came around to join him.

The copter gave a sudden lurch as it took that moment to start lifting off. Landon had just grabbed hold of Kaylee's hand and had wrapped his other hand around one metal support when a fiery pain erupted throughout his body. He barely had time to gasp at the intensity of all the pain and vaguely saw his own hand slip from where it had been on the door edge before the world turned black.

12

Jamie took a deep breath and forced her shaking hands to slow until she had control of them once more as she stood over another patient bed, her hands poised to finish re-stitching one soldier's wounds that had loosened during all the transfers from the previous base, to and from the helicopter, and back into the new medical ward they were in.

The air was thankfully silent from the sound of gunfire, but Jamie's ears were straining for any hint of incoming aircraft, other helicopters. 'They couldn't have been that much further behind us, could they? Could something have happened?' She took in another breath in an attempt to center herself in the moment, bring her focus back on the patient in front of her. 'Come on, Jamie, focus! This is your patient. Worrying about Landon is not going to help this soldier one bit,' she scolded herself.

She looked up to see Janine giving her a compassionate look, understanding Jamie's worry. Kindly, she didn't say anything but bowed her head towards the patient laying between them. Jamie nodded and focused on strengthening the stitches for the next few moments and making sure there was no leak before moving on to check on her other patients, Devin and Janine alternately prepping her with updates on the patients she had been attending to at the prior base. 'At least there's more room here to move around.'

'How many times have I gone in and out of those gates without a second thought, thinking that those walls would protect the people inside? Was it foolish to even think that those walls couldn't be breached? If anything, it was wishful thinking.'

She allowed herself one more quiet sigh before she forcefully pushed anymore thoughts regarding Landon and the war outside from her mind. A quick glance around showed that she had a handful more patients to check on before her meeting with the rest of the medical staff here to get oriented with the location and assimilated into the team.

Countless hours later, a glance at a nearby clock said that it was past midnight. Jamie finally found herself laying down on a free cot in the med staff quarters, no permanent bed having been assigned to her yet in their rushed arrival. It only seemed a matter of moments though of sleep before she felt a hand gently shaking her awake. She gave a start and sat up in bed, disoriented and realizing it was still dark out. The clock said sunrise was still an hour away. "I thought I pulled a later shift," she said, rubbing her eyes as she found Dr. Fong standing next to her cot.

"Jamie, it's Landon..."

Immediately, she was awake and out of bed, following her colleague back into the medical ward. Even at a distance, she spotted Adrian's tall form slumped in a chair, his head in his hands and a leg freshly bandaged.

"Adrian?" she barely noticed calling to him and

he tiredly raised a head at their approach. Her intent was on the section of the room that had been partitioned separately by a draped sheet. Even as she reached a hand to draw away the curtain, she felt Dr. Fong stop her from continuing on. "What?"

He shook his head. "I'm sorry, Jamie. I should have told you sooner, but he's in surgery right now."

"How bad?" The sinking feeling she'd had since they left her cot grew.

"Bad."

The word took awhile to process, but she was doing her best to deny it, shaking her head. "But I didn't hear any helicopters..."

"The helicopters didn't make it."

Jamie turned to Adrian, his eyes bloodshot and glistening with yet more unshed tears. "But how..."

"There were short range missiles or something. The copter in front of us exploded. A lot of the shrapnel hit ours too. Landon was still outside. He was the last one getting on. He was – " Adrian cut off, his throat thick with emotion and he squeezed his eyes shut, as if trying to erase the images that were undoubtedly replaying over and over in his head that moment.

"But how..."

"The copter was damaged but flyable. The team was able to get airborne but couldn't make it back all the way here. A rescue team was sent as soon as we were able to retrieve their location," Dr. Fong supplied when Adrian couldn't continue.

"It's been over a day..."

"The point is they made it."

She was already shaking her head. "No, I meant it's been over a day with Landon being that hurt. His chances..."

It was her turn to cut off as the reality of it all suddenly fell on her like a weight. Her knees buckled and Dr. Fong and Adrian both jumped to keep her from falling all the way to the floor. They settled her in the chair Adrian had vacated, but Jamie's eyes stayed on her colleague's face. "Be honest. His chances...?"

A pained expression and a shake of his head gave her more information than her mind could hope to process at that point. She closed her eyes and tilted her head back, her tears finally spilling over. Vaguely, she was aware of her tight grip on each man's hand still, needing their strength as her fight for control snapped. Comforting words fell on deaf ears as she prayed with all her strength that Landon would be okay, and her ears focused in on the hum of the machinery nearby, the only indication she knew that Landon was still alive.

As if in mockery though, just as she was focusing on the constant beeping, the sudden appearance of the shrill sound of the heart monitor going still came from behind the curtain. This time, neither man could not hold Jamie back. She tore through the curtained barrier, ignoring the startled glances of the surgeon and nurses there. "Landon!" She pushed her way to the head of the bed and grabbed a hand, ignoring the blood and dirt still caked onto his skin. "Landon? Landon! It's me, honey. It's Jamie! Don't go, oh please don't go!" she was screaming into his ear, her head bending down so their foreheads touched. "Landon, please, please stay. I'm here! Don't leave me!"

Even as the medical team rushed to do their duty and save the life in front of them, she fiercely clung to his side, yelling her encouragement to him, trying to keep him around a moment longer.

The heart monitor responded, giving them a beat, and then another. "Landon?" Jamie was afraid to let go of the hand. "Landon, please, you can make it through this..."

Amazingly, she watched as her husband opened his eyes and looked to her. Green eyes twinkled for a moment and she could swear he attempted a smile, a familiar crinkling around his eyes forming and causing her heart to warm. That hope in her heart left as quickly as it came as she watched those green eyes shut once more and the beep of the heart monitor reverted back to its drawn out siren.

This time, she allowed herself to be pushed back and aside, giving the staff more room to work. She lost her grip of his hand in the bustle, backing up more and more until she came against a solid wall. Slowly, she sank down and curled herself up into as tight a ball as she could, the image of Landon's shredded body laying on the table feet from her burned into her head and the long wail of the heart monitor continuing its chorus in the background.

13

"Jamie, honey, we're here."

Jamie blinked her eyes and realized that her mom was right. They'd arrived where Adrian and Caleb had organized a memorial for their fallen friends. Numbly, she got out of the car and allowed her father to take an arm and lead her in. It had been like that since she'd come back after the war had officially ended. Her parents had flown in specifically to meet her at the airport and settle her at home. But she'd gone on with her days in a trance, her mind still aching with the loss, his presence everywhere in the house they'd shared and filled with testaments to their love. How she had managed to outlast the war made her wonder, but then, she'd had a task, a job at hand, to save other lives, other people's loved ones... Back at home now, she was on indefinite leave, mending a broken heart.

Landon's body had long since been transported stateside and buried, a funeral held while she'd still been deployed. Her parents had taken her to the cemetery every day since she'd come home, spending most of the day there on that first visit. Most of the time, they were alone. Sometimes, they'd run into a mourning fan – how they had found the plot was beyond her, but still, it helped her as she spoke with those fans, sharing short stories.

But here, today, at the church, this would be the first time she'd seen Landon's family, his bandmates, his friends, their friends…

"Jamie, you're here!"

She turned and was quickly embraced by an Asian woman. "Anne, how are you?"

"Oh, Jamie, I'm so sorry for your loss."

And so it started. The tears she'd been holding back on in her numbed state spilled over anew as friends and family greeted her and she them, comforting each other prior to the service. She was sure the service itself was lovely, but truthfully, she remembered little of it, sitting between her parents and Landon's, who'd also come in for the occasion. At least she hadn't been paying attention until Adrian walked up to the podium to give a few words, limping a little still from the most serious wound he'd earned on the field.

'No,' she corrected herself. 'That's just physical. The heart of that man has been broken in a deeper way, a wound more substantial than any doctor could heal on a visit to the operating room.'

Adrian gave a nervous cough, suddenly looking younger and unsure of himself as he gazed at the people before him. Looking into his eyes though, Jamie saw that rather than nervousness though, there was a weariness in Adrian's gaze that spoke of having to live through the hardship of war. She'd seen it countless times before and it broke her heart to see it in such a close friend. She watched the man's hands shaking as he unfolded a piece of paper that he'd been holding onto. He stared at it hard, as if willing it to give him the strength he needed to say what he'd come up to say. Jamie's heart ached even more for him, understanding the pain.

"I lost three brothers this year, and a part of me has gone with each of them in their passing. Not a day goes by that I remember Hudson's goofiness, Luke's upbeat nature, or Landon's down to earth goodness. There isn't a moment when I can forget the fun and excitement we all shared in first coming together as a group, performing, recording, touring. We shared our triumphs, we shared our joys, we knew each other's struggles. I can still see in my mind Hudson and Luke running after each other after their latest pranks backstage and Landon just standing by shaking his head.

"It was bittersweet coming back together once more in a different way than any of us could have expected. Serving with them in a war that will hopefully end all wars, it was an honor and a privilege to have served alongside of them. We fought together, ate together, still joked around together... And yet they didn't get to come home with me, and that breaks my heart. It's not fair that Hudson will never get to sing another love song to Bridget, or that Luke won't get the chance to watch his little girls grow up, or Landon..." He stopped a moment, catching Jamie's eyes. "Or that Landon will never be able to say in person ever again how much he adored and loved you, Jamie.

"My brothers and I wrote letters back to our loved ones just in case anything happened to us. Jamie held onto those for us until the time was necessary that those be sent. What I don't think she knew was that Landon had written one such letter for her too, and I've been holding onto it until now, at Landon's request. It was his request too that I read it aloud here and now because honestly, he didn't want you to be alone when you first read it. May I?"

Tears slowly streaming down her face, and her emotions running wildly all over the place, she gave a small nod, even as her mom squeezed her hand a little tighter in support. He took out a worn looking envelope from inside his jacket and took out the letter inside.

"My dearest Jamie, if you're hearing this, then the unfortunate has happened and I have had to leave your side for the time being. Words cannot express how sorry I am for not being with you now, especially at a time you need it most — you know this was never my intention. To love and hold you in my arms, to kiss you good morning and good night, to comfort you in your sadness and sickness, and share in your joys and future accomplishments, I committed to do all that and more with you for life. Those were my hopes and dreams, and my heart breaks just thinking that, for now, it won't be so.

"My dear, I asked Adrian to read this letter to you at a time when you'd be surrounded by family and friends who love you. I didn't want you to be alone, but truthfully, I don't think you'll ever be alone. You are blessed to have surrounded yourself with good people. I know this because I was blessed to share part of my life with you. I was blessed the day you walked into my life — how thankful I was to able to catch your eye from across the café. I was blessed the day you agreed to go out to

dinner with me, even after you realized who I was and learned about my boyband history and the craziness that held in the past. I was blessed when you accepted my ring as my vow to forever love and support and cherish you, and I was blessed the day we officially made that vow a reality. In short, my life had already been a blessed one, but having you to share it with makes me the luckiest guy I know.

"Jamie, beloved, thank you for the many blessings you have given me. I will always, always love you. Your Landon"

Adrian folded the letter and placed it back into its envelope before stepping down and walking over to Jamie to present it. She stood and embraced him strongly, both crying tears for a man they'd both cared for deeply. "Thanks, Adrian," she whispered as he gave her the envelope. Before she could take her hand away though, he held on a moment longer, drawing out of his pocket a small box and placing that in her hand too. She gave a puzzled look.

"From Landon too, for later." He squeezed her hand one more time before going to take his seat next to Katie.

Later that night, long after the service was over and they'd gone to the cemetery for her daily visit, Jamie found herself in the quiet of her bedroom holding onto the small jewelry box Adrian had given her earlier. The letter was out and open, sitting next to her on the bed alongside a few used tissues. Gently, she opened the grey-silver box and felt the tears spring up into her eyes once more as she gazed at the bracelet inside.

Gingerly, she drew out the delicate chain from the box and stared at the simple plumeria charms dangling from it. Instantly, a cherished memory of the two walking hand in hand on a beach in Oahu when they'd been still been dating came to mind.

"You know, it's kinda sad you can't see the stars out here. I'm sure it would be so beautiful," Jamie said as her eyes strayed upwards, searching the skies.

"Who needs the stars when I'm already looking at the brightest, most beautiful thing around right now?"

Jamie laughed. "Flirt, you lie!"

Eyes twinkling, he gently tugged her closer and she easily fit herself to his side. He kissed the side of her head. "Not when it comes to you and your beauty. You know how lucky I am to be here with you right now?"

"Well, considering this trip was entirely last minute, yes, I know it's amazing we're even here right now."

"It's more than that, Jamie, and you know it. We could be in the middle of a desert and I'd still think I was the luckiest guy alive because you are here beside me, understanding me in ways no one else has ever done before."

"Well coming from so much time in the desert, I'm not going to complain about this beautiful change in scenery."

"Uh huh, and what about me?"

"What about you? You're just a bonus," she teased. "A very handsome bonus who offers a balance between the craziness of all I do at the hospital and the rest of my boring life."

Landon scoffed. "I would hardly call your life boring. Between your volunteering missions and expeditions and marathons, it's hard to believe you're okay with boring, old me."

"Balance, dear. You've had your share of excitement and traveling and doing what you love to do with the extra bonus of having people throwing themselves at your feet night after night."

"I've gotta say, that wasn't always fun but it sure was memorable."

"Would you do it all again if you had the chance?"

"In a heartbeat, yes. All of that has made me who I am today, just as your experiences have made you the woman walking beside me today. I can't trade it, nor do I want to."

"So you're saying there's no crazy stuff in your past you don't regret?"

"I'm guilty of perhaps not making the wisest choices every moment of my life," he shrugged a little. "But that's how I learn, how I grow. What I don't want to be guilty of though, is letting any opportunity to make my life better pass me by."

"And how do you do that?" she asked as Landon stopped their walk and he stood in front of her, taking her hands in his.

"Take it one step at a time," he replied, stooping down a little to give her a sweet kiss. Stepping back then but not letting go of her hands, he seemed to suddenly notice the plumeria tucked in her hair. "For example, would you mind if I move that flower to sit over your left ear?" At the puzzled look on her face, he explained even as he gently moved the flower for her. "Haven't you heard that it's tradition to place the flower over the left ear if you're taken?"

Jamie's heart thudded at the sudden change in topic. "What are you saying, Landon? To be taken I thought

85

meant to be married in this culture."

"Does being engaged count?"

She blinked in surprise. "Isn't there something else that usually goes along with being engaged?"

"You mean this?" Landon let go of one hand to pull out a small box from one pocket. Before Jamie could fully comprehend what was happening, Landon was down on one bended knee with a ring glinting up at her. "Jamie, love, would you do me the honor of being my wife? I cannot imagine life being as full and rich without you at my side every step of the way."

For Jamie, saying yes that night had meant the end of one chapter of her life, where coming into her own and learning to live life on her own terms had reigned. That night started a new chapter where she committed herself to embracing life and sharing its abundance with the man she loved. Every day together had been one of possibility, and every experience they'd shared was special and worth it. And now, with more plumerias given to her from the man she'd shared so much with, she knew he was reminding her of all the possibilities life could and would still bring to her.

With grateful heart, Jamie fastened the bracelet around her left wrist and unfolded the note that had been tucked in the jewelry box with the bracelet.

"I love you, Jamie, now and always."

With a glance over at their wedding portrait, which was sitting on her bedside table, she finally gave a smile and offered a silent prayer of thanks and gratitude before laying down in bed. Her heart was feeling a touch lighter than it had in many days, all due to the gentle reminder that life was still waiting for her to experience it even more.

And for now, that was enough.

IN GRATITUDE

For those who have given of themselves into service to protect those left behind in times of war and conflict, I honor and thank you for your sacrifices.

Also, my sincerest thanks to you for taking your time to read through this latest attempt at fiction. I would greatly appreciate it if you took a moment to leave an honest review on Amazon and share with others via social media:

https://www.amazon.com/-/e/B078M9S7S1

ABOUT THE AUTHOR

M. A. VALDELLON is a dreamer at heart.

When she's not immersed in the literary world, she can often be found playing and creating with crystals and music, cuddling with her furry loved ones, enjoying hot chocolate, and mentoring students and patients on their eyes and health in the Bay Area, California.

With three books already published and at least three more on the way, M. A. is certainly keeping herself out of trouble, but is not too busy as to be unavailable. You can contact her by email directly on her website, http://melissavaldellon.com/, and she will personally get back to you shortly.

Her next fiction, *To Be Broken*, will be released summer 2018.